Every new generation of children is enthralled by the famous stories in our Well Loved Tales series. Younger ones love to have the story read to them. Older children will enjoy the exciting stories in an easy-to-read text.

British Library Cataloguing in Publication Data
Randall, Ronne
  The twelve dancing princesses.—(Well Loved Tales).
  I. Title   II. Papps, Patricia
  III. Grimm, Jacob. Zertanzte Schuhe   IV. Series
  813'.54[J]   PZ8
  ISBN 0-7214-1053-7

First edition

Published by Ladybird Books Ltd Loughborough Leicestershire UK
Ladybird Books Inc Lewiston Maine 04240 USA

© LADYBIRD BOOKS LTD MCMLXXXVII

Printed in England

The Twelve Dancing Princesses

retold for easy reading
by RONNE PELTZMAN RANDALL

illustrated by PATRICIA PAPPS

Ladybird Books

Once there was a king who had
twelve beautiful daughters. They all
slept in the same room, and when

they went to bed each night, the
king locked and bolted their door.

But every morning when the king opened their door, he found that the princesses' shoes were completely worn through.

"How can this be?" the king wondered. "What do my daughters do each night?" No one knew.

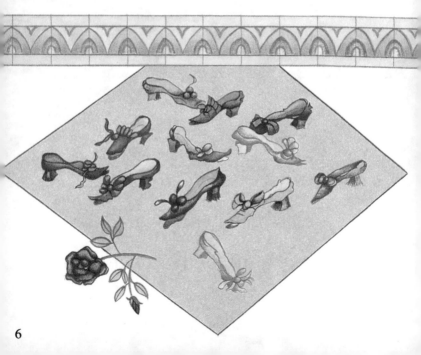

7

At last the king announced that anyone who could find out how his daughters wore out their shoes could choose one of the princesses to be his wife.

The very next day a young prince
came to try his luck.

The prince was taken to a room
next to the princesses' bedroom,
and was told to keep watch. So that
he could see what the princesses

did, the door to their room was left open.

Before long the prince's eyelids grew heavy. He tried hard to stay awake, but he couldn't.

When the prince woke up the next
morning, the princesses' shoes were
again worn through. The prince
had failed, and he had to leave the
palace.

Many more young men came and
tried their luck, but none
succeeded.

One day a poor soldier decided to try and learn the princesses' secret. On his way to the palace, he met an old woman.

"I can help you," she said. "If
you want to find out where the
princesses go and what they do,
don't drink anything they bring
you. Just pretend to fall fast
asleep."

Then she gave him a cloak. "When you put this on, you will be invisible," she said. "You'll be able to follow the princesses wherever they go."

So the soldier made his way to the
palace. Like the others before him,
he was taken to a room next to the

princesses'. Before long, the eldest

princess came in and gave him

some wine.

Remembering what the old woman
had told him, the soldier only
pretended to drink the wine.

Then he lay down, and after a little
while he began to snore as if he
were asleep.

When the princesses heard him, they got up and dressed in their finest clothes and jewels. When

they were all ready, they looked at the soldier again. He was still snoring. "We are safe," said the eldest princess.

The eldest princess then went to
her bed and tapped on it. It sank
into the floor and became a wide
staircase. One by one, all the
princesses went down the stairs.

The soldier, who had seen everything, didn't waste a minute. He threw the magic cloak over his shoulders and followed the princesses.

At the bottom of the stairs, there was a row of splendid trees. The leaves were all silver, and they sparkled and glittered.

"I'd better take something to prove where I've been," thought the soldier. He broke off one of the branches and hid it under his cloak.

Next they came to a row of trees
with leaves of gold.

Once again the soldier thought,
"I'd better take something back
with me," and he broke off a
golden branch.

Finally they came to a row of trees
with leaves of pure shimmering
diamonds. The soldier took one of
these branches, too.

On and on the princesses went,

until they came to a wide river.

Twelve boats were waiting at the

bank, with a handsome prince in each one. Each prince helped a princess into his boat.

The soldier got into the last boat,
with the youngest princess. "I don't

know why," said her prince,
"but the boat seems very heavy
tonight. I have to row with all my
strength just to make it move!"

On the other side of the river there
was a magnificent palace. It was

ablaze with lights, and lively music came from within. Everyone went inside.

There, in a vast ballroom, each
prince danced with his princess,
whirling and twirling to the music
of trumpets and drums. They

danced and danced, until three in the morning. Then all the princesses' shoes were worn through, and they had to stop.

The princes rowed them back
across the river. This time the
soldier sat in the first boat, with
the eldest princess. On the bank,

the princesses said goodbye to their
princes, and promised to come
again the following night.

When they reached the staircase,
the soldier ran on ahead. He
quickly climbed into his bed,
hiding the three branches under his
pillow. By the time the princesses

came in, his eyes were closed and
he was snoring loudly once again.

"No need to worry about him,"
said the eldest princess.

The princesses put away their fine
clothes and jewels. Then they put
their worn-out shoes under their
beds and went to sleep.

The next morning the soldier went
to the king.

"Now," said the king, "can you
tell me what my daughters have
been doing every night?"

"Yes," replied the soldier. "They have been dancing with twelve princes in an underground palace." He told the king everything that had happened, and showed him the three branches.

The king sent for his daughters and asked them whether the soldier was telling the truth. Though they were sorry that their secret had been discovered, they knew they could not lie. "Yes," they said. "It is true."

So the king asked the soldier which
princess he wanted to marry. The
soldier chose the eldest, and they

lived happily ever after. But the
twelve princesses never again went
dancing in the magnificent
underground palace.